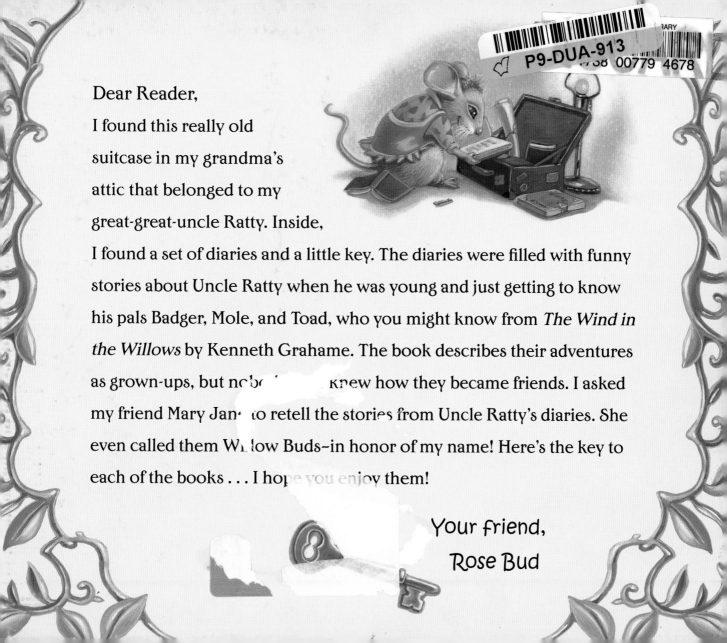

P9-DUA-913
⁊38 00779 4678
RARY

Dear Reader,

I found this really old
suitcase in my grandma's
attic that belonged to my
great-great-uncle Ratty. Inside,
I found a set of diaries and a little key. The diaries were filled with funny
stories about Uncle Ratty when he was young and just getting to know
his pals Badger, Mole, and Toad, who you might know from *The Wind in
the Willows* by Kenneth Grahame. The book describes their adventures
as grown-ups, but nobody knew how they became friends. I asked
my friend Mary Jane to retell the stories from Uncle Ratty's diaries. She
even called them Willow Buds—in honor of my name! Here's the key to
each of the books . . . I hope you enjoy them!

Your friend,
Rose Bud

Willow Buds

The Tale of
Toad and Badger

written and illustrated by

Mary Jane Begin

LITTLE, BROWN AND COMPANY

New York ∙ Boston

DISCARD

EL DORADO COUNTY LIBRARY
345 FAIR LANE
PLACERVILLE, CA 95667

To my brother, Chuck,
who learned how to sew.

Copyright © 2008 by Mary Jane Begin

Hand lettering by Leah Palmer Preiss

All rights reserved. Except as permitted under the U.S. Copyright Act of 1976, no part of this publication may be reproduced, distributed, or transmitted in any form or by any means, or stored in a database or retrieval system, without the prior written permission of the publisher.

Little, Brown and Company
Hachette Book Group USA
237 Park Avenue, New York, NY 10017
Visit our Web site at www.lb-kids.com

First Edition: April 2008

ISBN-10: 0316013528
ISBN-13: 9780316013529

10 9 8 7 6 5 4 3 2 1

Book design by Alison Impey

SC

Printed in China

The illustrations for this book were done in watercolor and pastel on Canson paper.
The text was set in Edwardian.

January 28, 1922

Dear Diary,

Badger just told me the most amusing story about the first time he met our dear friend Toady. I was in stitches! Badger and Toad are just like brothers— they love each other but they don't always get along. I must write it all down before I forget anything.

Very truly yours,
Ratty

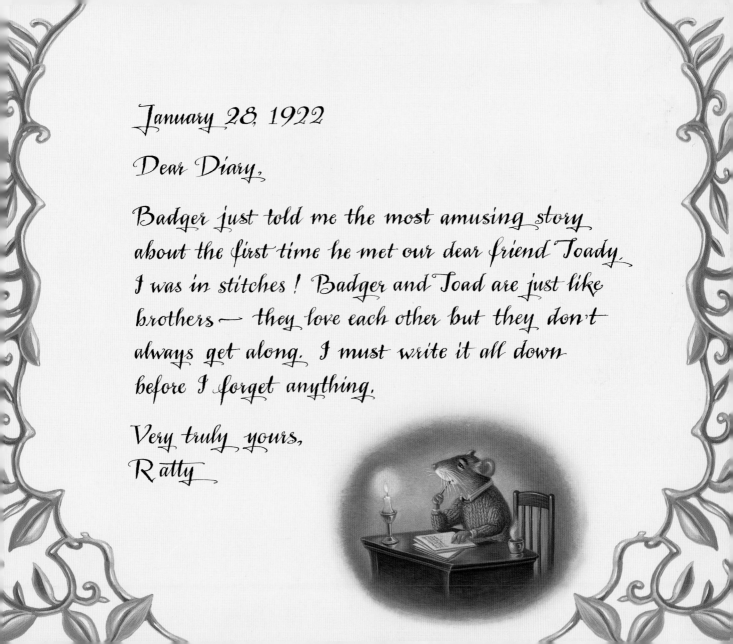

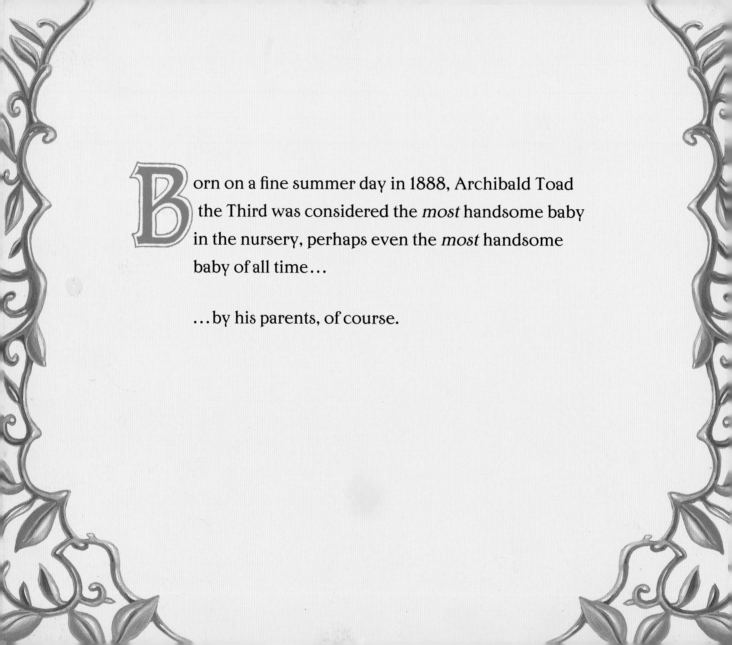

Born on a fine summer day in 1888, Archibald Toad the Third was considered the *most* handsome baby in the nursery, perhaps even the *most* handsome baby of all time…

…by his parents, of course.

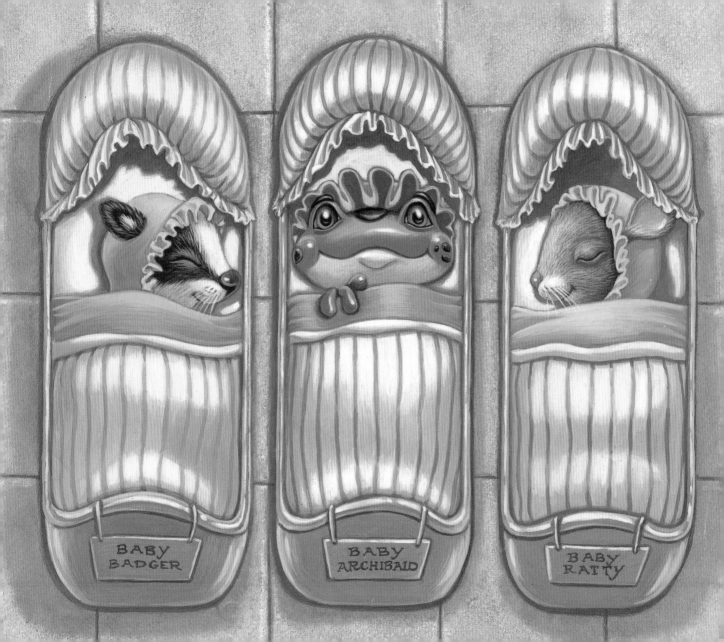

BABY
BADGER

BABY
ARCHIBALD

BABY
RATTY

Before long, he became known as "Toady," for it was much easier to say, "Toady, don't touch that!" or "Toady, put that down!" than "Archibald Toad the Third, don't throw your spinach!"

As Toady grew, Mr. and Mrs. Toad decided to hire a nanny to look after him. The sour-faced Mrs. Nag lasted one week.

Mrs. Hogg, who snored and drooled when she napped, lasted only one day.

And Miss Wanda Weasel liked shiny things that didn't belong to her. She lasted exactly one hour.

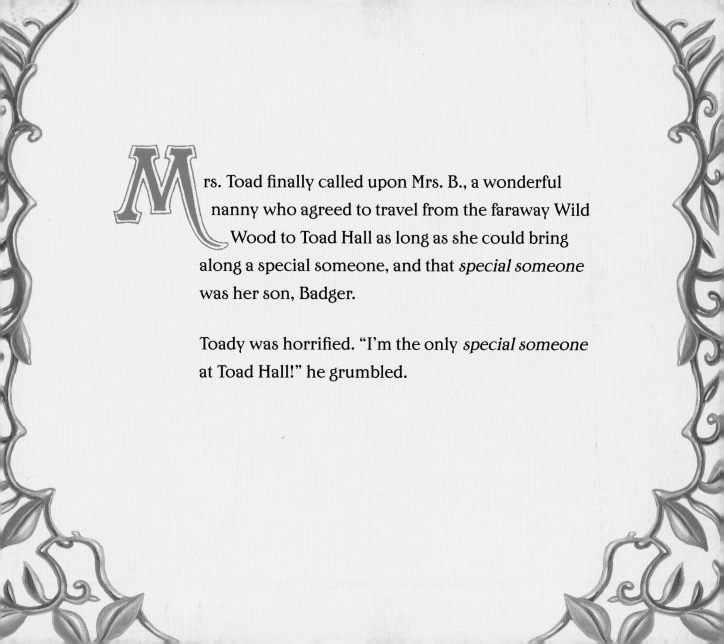

Mrs. Toad finally called upon Mrs. B., a wonderful nanny who agreed to travel from the faraway Wild Wood to Toad Hall as long as she could bring along a special someone, and that *special someone* was her son, Badger.

Toady was horrified. "I'm the only *special someone* at Toad Hall!" he grumbled.

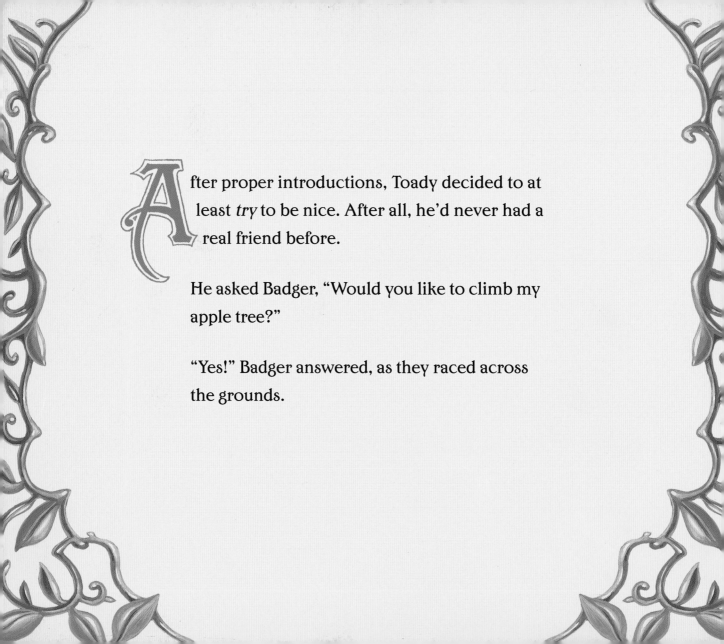

After proper introductions, Toady decided to at least *try* to be nice. After all, he'd never had a real friend before.

He asked Badger, "Would you like to climb my apple tree?"

"Yes!" Badger answered, as they raced across the grounds.

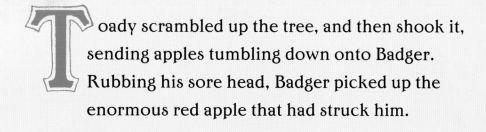

oady scrambled up the tree, and then shook it, sending apples tumbling down onto Badger. Rubbing his sore head, Badger picked up the enormous red apple that had struck him.

"You took the one *I* wanted!" Toady declared, and stomped back to the house.

Badger followed, crunching his apple loudly.

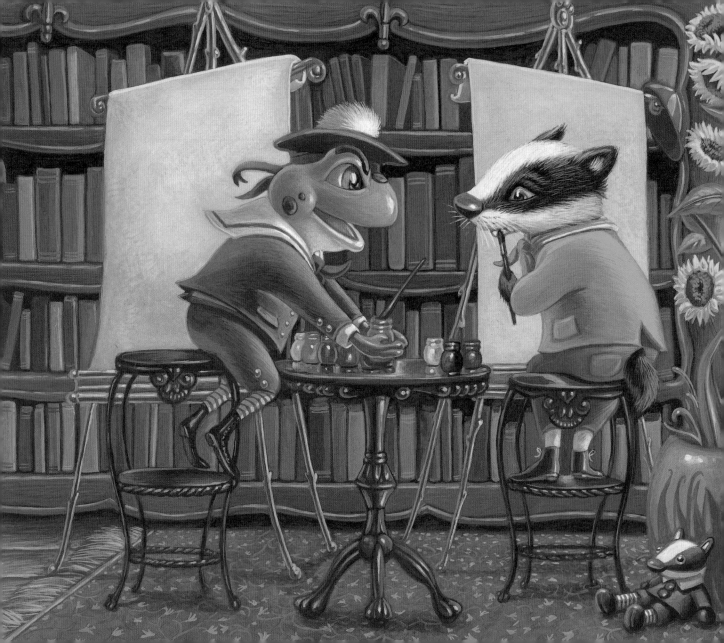

As Mrs. B. prepared lettuce and peanut butter sandwiches for lunch, Toady and Badger sat down to paint. "*These* are mine, and *those* are yours," announced Toady, pulling most of the paint cups to his side of the table.

As Badger finished his painting, he remarked, "These are the *perfect* colors for painting a badger!"

Toady stuck out his tongue.

After lunch, the boys went to play in Toady's room. "You might break my toys," Toady told Badger, "so you'd better just play with your old stuffed dolly."

"It's *not* a stuffed dolly, it's Andy," said Badger. "My mom made him and he's the *best* toy in the world!"

By naptime, Badger and Toady were not speaking to each other. After Mrs. B. tucked the boys in, Toady crept across the room and lifted Andy from Badger's side.

With a great

SWOOSH!

Toady swung Andy high up
onto a bookshelf.

One of Andy's legs could still be seen, so Toady reached for it. He tugged, but it didn't budge. He tugged harder.

He tugged *very* hard and there was a terrible

RRRRRRRIPP!

"O h, nooo…" groaned Toady, feeling sick. He pulled the two sides of Andy toward him, and then stuffed the toy under the bookshelf.

"Where's Andy?" Badger cried when he awoke, searching high and low for his beloved toy.

Then he reached under the bookshelf.

Toady could see Badger's shoulders quivering.

No one said a word.

"I didn't mean it!" wailed Toady. "I was only trying to hide Andy because I was mad at you!"

"Why? What did *I* do?" asked Badger.

"It's just that I've never had to share Toad Hall until now," Toady answered quietly. "I'm sorry."

"Are you *really* sorry or just *saying* it?" Badger asked.

"I'm *really* sorry!" answered Toady as he tenderly touched Andy's ear. "Wait…I have an idea! Let's sew him back together!"

Toady raced out the door to get the sewing basket. They tried to sew, but Toady poked himself twice with the needle, and Badger stitched his shirt to the bedspread.

Toady and Badger carefully carried Andy to Mrs. B. She showed the boys how to thread the needle, where to sew the seam, and when to tie the knot. Together, they made Andy whole again.

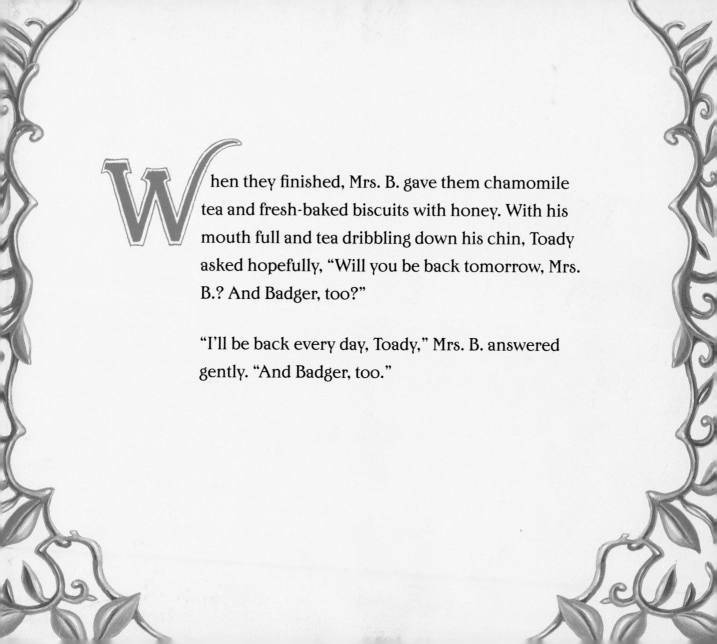

When they finished, Mrs. B. gave them chamomile tea and fresh-baked biscuits with honey. With his mouth full and tea dribbling down his chin, Toady asked hopefully, "Will you be back tomorrow, Mrs. B.? And Badger, too?"

"I'll be back every day, Toady," Mrs. B. answered gently. "And Badger, too."

NOV 1 9 2008

SOUTH LAKE TAHOE

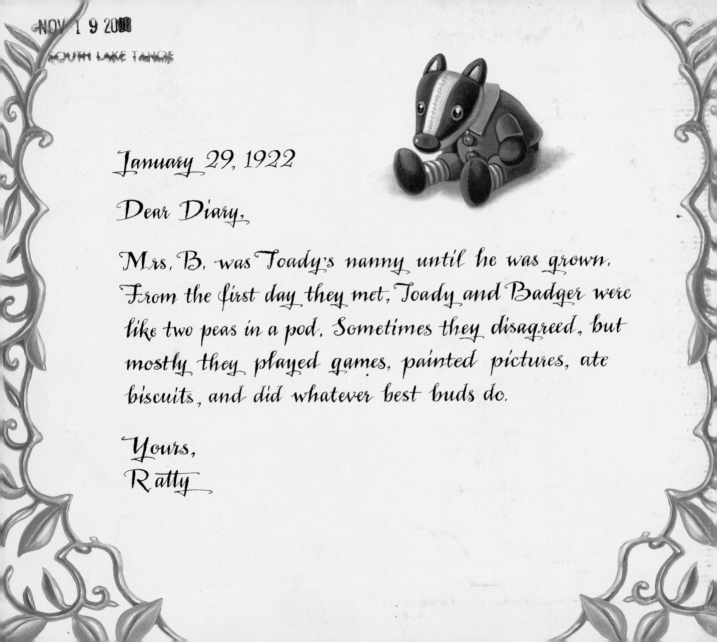

January 29, 1922

Dear Diary,

Mrs. B. was Toady's nanny until he was grown. From the first day they met, Toady and Badger were like two peas in a pod. Sometimes they disagreed, but mostly they played games, painted pictures, ate biscuits, and did whatever best buds do.

Yours,
Ratty